Riot Act

Riot Act

Diane Tullson

orca soundings

ORCA BOOK PUBLISHERS

Library and Archives Canada Cataloguing in Publication

Tullson, Diane, 1958-
Riot act / Diane Tullson.

(Orca soundings)
Issued also in an electronic format.
ISBN 978-1-4598-0140-0 (BOUND).--ISBN 978-1-4598-0139-4 (PBK.)

I. Title. II. Series: Orca soundings.
PS8589.U6055R56 2012 JC813'.6 C2011-907849-X

First published in the United States, 2012
Library of Congress Control Number: 2011943736

Summary: Daniel and his friend are caught up in a postgame riot.

Orca Book Publishers is dedicated to preserving the environment and has printed this book on paper certified by the Forest Stewardship Council.®

Orca Book Publishers gratefully acknowledges the support for its publishing programs provided by the following agencies: the Government of Canada through the Canada Book Fund and the Canada Council for the Arts, and the Province of British Columbia through the BC Arts Council and the Book Publishing Tax Credit.

Cover photography by dreamstime.com

ORCA BOOK PUBLISHERS
PO Box 5626, Stn. B
Victoria, BC Canada
V8R 6S4

ORCA BOOK PUBLISHERS
PO Box 468
Custer, WA USA
98240-0468

www.orcabook.com
Printed and bound in Canada.

15 14 13 12 • 4 3 2 1

For Chris, with love.

Chapter One

I drop the hood down on Dad's F-150. "Oil is good." Dad's had the truck for ten years, and it wasn't new when he got it, but we've kept it in pristine condition.

He says, "Brakes will need doing soon."

"Let's do them before I buy the truck." I fake-punch him in the arm.

"Ha ha. Maybe you'll go halfers on the parts."

"Maybe I will. I'm making good money this summer."

"You'll need it." He tosses a folded police uniform shirt onto the seat. "I almost feel guilty selling you such an old truck."

"No way. When I have the truck, my boss says he'll give me some framing work." I give the hood paint a quick polish. "I won't miss pushing a broom."

"You'll need your own tools."

"I know. I'll save for those too."

"Must be good work in the construction trade." He smiles. "I guess I don't have to worry about you."

"That's right. Just keep saving your pennies, Dad, because as soon as you buy your new truck, I'm buying this one."

"I'll get right on that." He slides in behind the wheel. "I'm sure I'll get some overtime tonight." He shakes his head. "I'd like to know who had the bright idea to set up a live site right in the downtown core. Buildings all sides—it's like a concrete cave." He turns the key, and the truck rumbles to life. "You'll be at Nick's tonight to watch the game?"

"Uh-huh." I fake-punch him again and grin. "You don't have to worry about me."

He gives me a look. "I'm serious, Daniel."

"Dad, relax. When have I ever been anything less than a perfect son?"

He rolls his eyes. "Actions speak louder than words." His gaze drops. "How's your mother?"

Yeah, speaking of actions. I was nine when she moved out. She said it was just a trial separation and that she needed some distance. This week she's in Hawaii, a great last-minute deal, she told me. I guess she's getting some distance. I make my voice cheerful and say, "Good. Mom is good. She says to say hi."

At Nick's house, the TV is on, of course. I can hear it even before I open the front door. His grandmother is sitting in her chair in the living room, the remote on the armrest beside her, along with her hearing aid. She'd rather turn up the volume. I call, "Hey, Gram!"

She looks over at me and grins. Fine lines fan out from the corners of her eyes. She waves and cries, "Hi, Daniel!" The sleeve of her sweater slips to her elbow. I give her a thumbs-up and follow the aroma of supper into the kitchen.

Nick's older sister stands at the stove, flipping burgers. She used to babysit me after my mom left. I even slept here sometimes when Dad was on night shift.

"Hey, Mia. Your turn to cook dinner?"

She hands me a plate of supper. "Nick's actually, but he just got home from work and I told him he'd better get his homework done before the game."

"You're going to make a great mother someday," I say.

Mia says, "I can wait awhile for that, thanks very much."

Sebastian, their terror of a little brother, just about knocks his chair over as he runs to me. He tugs on my hand. "Sit with me, okay? Mia's going to make popcorn for the game. And she bought us Pepsi."

I glance at the table to see only four places set. "Your parents working?"

Mia says, "They're cleaning two buildings this week. They won't be home until after midnight."

I pull Sebastian into a gentle headlock. "Popcorn and Pepsi. Sounds like a feast, but I think Nick and I are going downtown to watch."

Sebastian howls, "No!"

Mia gives me a look over her shoulder. "It's going to be crazy down there."

I tug Sebastian back to his spot at the table and take the chair next to his. I say to Mia, "How many years has it been since this city has played in the final? We weren't even born. History is being made tonight." I thump the table for effect. "We're going to be there."

She loads a burger onto Sebastian's plate. He squirts a stream of ketchup onto his burger and then turns it upside down to eat. He eats everything upside down. Ketchup gathers in the corners of his mouth. I say, "You look like a vampire, dude." He tries to catch it with his tongue, but ketchup drips onto the front of his shirt. I toss him a napkin and use another to wipe the worst off his shirt.

Mia has a spatula in one hand. The other hand is planted on her hip. She waves the spatula at me. "What if there's trouble? People are talking about a riot."

"Those people are morons." I eat the last of my burger. "My dad says they've put extra staff on. And anyway, Nick and I can take care of ourselves."

Around a mouthful of burger, Sebastian says, "I'm going to be a police officer too."

Mia is still looking at me. "Are you planning on drinking?"

"Who, us?" I grin.

She says, "You don't have to get stupid drunk, you know."

I'm about to laugh but stop when I see the look on her face. She says, "The two of you don't need much help to get stupid."

"Ouch," I say.

She stabs the spatula in my direction. "You stay together."

"We always do."

She turns her back to me, and I can see from the set of her shoulders that she's pissed about us going. Nick appears in the doorway. He has to duck his head as he enters the kitchen. Last year, before twelfth grade, Nick must have grown about a foot in all directions. He's wearing a team jersey. My dad got us each a jersey when the team made the quarterfinals. We've worn them every game day. Sebastian gets up from the table, wraps his arms around Nick's leg and says, "I want to go with you guys."

A low growl rumbles from Mia. Nick meets my eyes and grins. "Not this time," he says.

Sebastian's voice creeps toward tears. "Why can't I?"

Nick peels the boy off his leg and bends down so they're face-to-face. "You have to help Gram find the right station.

You look for us when they show the crowd, okay?" He gives me a quick glance and then takes off his jersey. Underneath it he's wearing his work shirt, a bright red T-shirt with *Shoe Barn* emblazoned on the front. He says to his brother, "You can wear my jersey tonight."

Sebastian's eyes widen. "Daniel's dad gave it to you." He stands in awe as Nick drops the jersey over his head and folds the sleeves up. It comes down to the kid's knees.

Nick says, "You wear it. For luck."

Mia says, "You'd better change out of that shirt. You'll need it for work tomorrow."

Nick says, "Maybe you'll cover my shift."

"Maybe I won't. I didn't get you that job just so I could work it. I've already done five shifts there this week. Go change your shirt."

I say, "He doesn't have time. We've got to go. People have been down there since this morning."

Nick says to Mia, "I'll wear one of yours tomorrow. Relax."

"Very funny, and don't tell me to relax."

Sebastian hugs his brother. I go over to the stove and nudge Mia in the hip. "We'll be fine. I promise, okay?"

She's known me since Nick and I were six. I can see in her eyes that she believes me.

Nick says, "Promise her what?"

I push him toward the door. He says, "Hey, I didn't eat!"

"We'll get something down there."

As we pass through the living room, we both call goodbye to his grandmother. She blows a kiss for each of us.

At the door I pause and look back. Sebastian is climbing onto the couch while balancing a huge glass of Pepsi. It doesn't occur to him to set the glass down first. Maybe he'll figure it out. I keep shoving Nick until we're through the door.

Chapter Two

"It looks like everyone had the same idea," Nick calls. "The game will be almost over by the time we get out of here."

He's ahead of me in the line for pizza. We got in line at the last intermission, and the game has already started again. A small, ancient wall-mount TV shows the game. The shop is crowded, and the line snakes around a couple of scarred tables toward the counter. It's been like this since we got down here. So many people. Office workers, families, guys like us—half the city has poured into the plaza where giant TV screens blare the game. Here in the pizza shop, a cooler with beer is chained closed. My dad told me that liquor sales in the plaza had been shut down so that people wouldn't get shit-faced. Security guys checked people as they came into the plaza, but no one patted us down. I readjust the bottle jammed in my waistband. Yeah, good luck keeping people from drinking.

The shop is seriously last century. The walls are papered with brown and orange roses, very nice, and the vinyl tile floor is orange-gold. But it's spotless, even the corners of the floor. Someone must take a toothbrush to it every night. A couple of guys come into the shop and start muscling in front of people. People were happier when we first got down here. But the game isn't going so well. The guys budge in front of a family standing behind me in the line. The man looks like he'd like to say something, but he just puts his arm over his daughter's shoulder. The girl looks about thirteen, so I get why the man is letting it go. But they've been waiting a long time. I jab the elbow of one of the guys. "Back there," I say, pointing to the end of the line. The guy looks me up and down. He's about the same size as me, but I hope he doesn't decide to take a swing. I'm calculating my chances when Nick turns around.

He says, "Daniel, I'm up next. What do you want?"

The guy looks up at Nick, pauses for about one second and then grabs his friend and moves toward the back of the line.

Behind the counter, two workers fly around, an old guy with a tiger tattoo on his hand and a girl, maybe our age. She's nice-looking, with dark hair tied in a knot at her neck. She wears an apron with her name embroidered on it. *Abbi*. She's bagging an order, making change, grabbing stuff out of a big refrigerator. The old guy wipes his forehead on his sleeve. I check the score on the TV. I don't know why I bother. I would have heard—the crowd goes nuts if we score. But no, we are still losing.

"Get me some chips." I hand Nick a bill. "I've got to take a leak."

Nick moves to the counter. The girl's eyes widen briefly. Nick gets that a lot. I say to her, "Hey, Abbi, washrooms in the back?"

She glances at me. "Sorry, it's only for customers."

I point to Nick and smile. "I'm with him."

Her gaze travels from me to Nick, and she nods. "Next to the alley door."

There's a line here too, no surprise. A woman gets in the line behind me. She's with a little kid. He's wearing an adult-sized jersey with the sleeves rolled up. The kid jiggles from foot to foot. Sebastian does that too when he has to pee. The washroom comes available, and I offer it to the woman. She thanks me about nine times as she pulls the kid in with her.

Back outside, it's not hard to find Nick's bright-red T-shirt. He hands me a can of Dr. Pepper.

"Where are my chips?" I say.

He shakes his head. "They're all out."

The can feels warm. "I don't even like Dr. Pepper."

"It's all they had."

"What did you get?"

He burps. "Two cans of Dr. Pepper."

"Nothing to eat?"

"Sold out of everything."

I turn to see the older worker hanging a Closed sign in the window. I hand Nick the can. "Fill your boots."

We push toward the middle of the crowd and squeeze in behind a couple. She has her head leaning on his shoulder. I pull the bottle from my waistband and take a swig, then hand it to Nick. He's already had a fair bit of his own, and he teeters as he drinks. The guy beside Nick is drinking a can of beer. I hear a man's voice right beside me, but the words don't register at first.

He says it again, and this time I hear. "I'll have that bottle."

I turn to see a cop in regular uniform wearing a yellow traffic vest. He stares at Nick, motioning with his hand that he wants the bottle. I don't recognize him, thank goodness. Nick must not hear, because he tips the bottle up and takes a big drink. The cop shoves in front of me and puts his hand on Nick's shoulder.

Nick just about chokes when he sees the cop.

The guy beside him starts to laugh. He must have spotted the cop, because he was able to get his beer out of sight.

Nick splutters, "Sorry, sir." He passes the cop the bottle cap, then the bottle.

The guy with the beer starts to boo, and others take it up. The cop's eyes dart in their direction, then all around him. He smiles, but it doesn't look real. I glance around too, hoping I don't see my dad. The cop takes the bottle and steps over to the curb. He pours it out into a storm drain and drops the empty bottle on top of a full trash can. I wait for him to come back and say something, but he turns and leaves. As soon as he's gone, Nick pulls his own bottle out of his pants and hands it to me.

"Sorry, man. You can have mine."

I wave it away. "It's okay. Keep it."

Nick shrugs and takes a drink. One of the guys claps him on the back, which makes him almost choke again. Another guy just about pisses himself, he finds this so funny. The couple in front tries to shift away from us, but there's hardly room to move. She says something to her boyfriend, and he shakes his head.

A groan lifts from the crowd. I look up at the screen in time to see the replay—they've scored again. A booing, jeering wave crashes on top of us. The guy who was laughing a minute ago is purple-faced now, jabbing his middle finger at the screen.

The girl tugs on her boyfriend's arm. She shouts over the sound of the crowd, "No way we'll win now. Let's go."

She's right. There's not enough time left for us to come back. But I can't believe it. We were supposed to bring home the cup. It was our turn.

An empty bottle of Captain Morgan smashes at my feet. I feel the glass hit my jeans. The guy who threw it is red-eyed and wild, punching his fist in the air, swearing at the other team.

The girl's eyes are like plates. "If we go now, maybe we won't have to wait for a train." She puts her arms around her boyfriend.

He turns and scans the crowd, maybe looking for an opening. But the people form a wall. The purple-faced guy pumps his fist in the guy's face. When the couple tries to push past him, he shoves the guy in the chest. The girl starts to say something, but her boyfriend shushes her.

Nick says, "I'm starving, man. Let's go."

His voice is slurred. I try to make a sliver of room for the couple to squeeze past.

The guy shoulders through, the girl hanging on to his belt behind him. Somehow they manage to move through the crowd as it closes around them.

I say to Nick, "We may as well wait. Once people start to move, we'll be able to get ahead of them."

Nick sighs and turns back to the screen. As he finishes the last of his booze, the buzzer sounds.

We've lost. I gape at the screen, waiting for some miracle do-over. But our team is headed for the dressing room, hanging their heads. The other team jumps on each other and cheers.

We lost. How did that happen? How did we lose?

The guy who threw the Captain Morgan bottle is crazed. He screams at the screen as if the other team can hear him. The cords in his neck stick out, and he's broken into a sweat. He climbs up on his buddy's shoulders. A crowd camera must pick him up, because there he is on the big screen, spit flying off his lips as he clearly mouths profanities. He sees himself on TV and hoots. His friends jump up and down, trying to get in the shot. The view moves back to the game, the other team with the cup. The guy gets down and grabs an almost empty bottle from his friend. He drains it, then hurls the bottle against the closest building. It smashes over the pizza shop sign, and people cheer. Someone takes his picture as if he's a celebrity. Other people throw bottles. At the edge of the crowd, people shield their faces against the breaking glass.

A guy starts up a chant slagging the other team, complete with ridiculous dance moves. Other people join in, and it becomes an obscene line dance. People laugh and cheer. Nick takes a place and, for a guy so drunk, performs an appallingly good disco routine.

He picks up an empty bottle and holds it like a microphone.

Someone from the crowd shouts, "Throw it!" Others take up the call, and it becomes a chant. "Throw it! Throw it!"

Nick weaves, unsteady on his feet. He doesn't even look where he's throwing, just lobs the bottle in a gigantic arc. It nails the window of the pizza shop and punches a hole in the glass. Shards rain onto the sidewalk. The crowd roars. I doubt he meant to hit the window, but Nick is an instant hero, and he grins.

Bottles are flying, and people move into the throng to avoid the glass, pushing against people who are trying to leave. Someone jostles me, and I shove him back.

A siren wails, and a police car noses between people. I grab Nick and pull him into the crowd. A guy throws a bottle at the car and two regular-uniform cops jump out. They try to wrestle the guy into the car, but the crowd seethes around them. People jeer. Somebody starts bouncing the trunk of the cop car.

My dad wouldn't be anywhere near this crowd, not with just one partner and not without gear. And no one is making it easy for these two cops. The crowd clusters around like they're watching a show. One cop says something into his mouthpiece, and it looks like the two are rethinking. They let the guy go, and the crowd cheers. The cop car is surrounded now, people at front and back, rocking it. The cops don't spend any time discussing it—they abandon the car and slip into the crowd. For a second I can see their yellow vests. Then they vanish.

Guys swarm the cop car. Someone kicks the side window. A bottle hits the windshield and shatters a round white target in the safety glass. A group of guys rips a newspaper box from the sidewalk and hurls it through the windshield. Pebbles of glass spray our feet. People hold their phones over the crowd to take pictures. Someone screams, and I turn to see what looks like a bottle flying into the cop car. There's a trail of smoke and then a weird pause, like the torch is taking a breath. Then the car bursts into flames.

Chapter Three

Black smoke bites my lungs. My air passages seem to close, and I gasp to get a breath. As I turn away from the police car, there's a whooshing sound and flames spill from the broken windows. People scramble back from the flames. It feels like my jersey is on fire, but it's not. The torched car, the cheering crowd—it's awful and scary, and weirdly fun, like we're in a virtual world. But the smoke is real—very real—and the rules have changed.

A guy steps in front of the car and poses, pointing to his shirt, which reads, *I'm here for the riot.* He's wearing sunglasses, and I wonder if he was the one who threw the torch. I don't know how he can stand so close to the burning car. Even away from it, my jeans are burning hot.

People start streaming away from the fire at the same time as others run to watch it burn. I grab Nick and join a pack of guys cutting through a parking lot. A few people sit in their cars, waiting to leave. The lot is jammed. Some drivers try to back up into the flow of people but get stopped. There's a Mini parked at the edge of the walkway with no one in it. Someone yells, "Tip the Mini!" Several guys put their shoulder to the car. Someone else yells,

"Get it rocking." They let the car fall, and when it recoils, they push it again.

They're actually getting air. My dad told me that when he was in college, he and his buddies carried a Ford Fiesta up the steps of the administration building. Carrying a Fiesta probably didn't really damage it. Flipping it might.

I'm glad my dad's truck isn't parked down here.

A skinny kid takes a spot at the side of the car. He can't weigh more than ninety pounds, and it makes me laugh to see him grunting and pushing. No way will they be able to tip the car. I yell, "Heave!" The tires lift a few inches off the ground. "Heave!"

Someone yells to Nick, "Get in there and push!"

He makes a move, but I grab his sleeve.

More guys throw their weight against the car. "Push!" The whole crowd seems to chant. "Push!"

Amazingly, the car is almost on its side, the whole underside showing.

"Push!"

The car tilts, teeters for an instant, then topples upside down.

How often do you get to see a car tipped over? People cheer. We dance around the turtled car, our hands in the air. I pull out my phone and shout to Nick, "I'll take your picture!"

He poses in front of the tipped car, his head thrown back and both middle fingers in the air. He's imitating the guy earlier who got on TV, and I can't stop laughing to take the picture. Behind him, people crawl up on the underside of the car. People hoot and cheer. Suddenly, every phone and camera seems pointed at a guy poking something into the window of the car. Someone yells, "Get out of the way!" That's when I see the guy shaking liquid inside the car. The guy wipes his hands on his jersey, and still I don't quite get it. All I can think is, Wow, if that is gas, wiping it on yourself is incredibly dumb. He touches a lighter to a rag and throws it in.

Nick and I stumble away. At first the interior of the car lights up red. Then smoke spills out. Flames lick over the underside of the car, growing hot on the grease. Overhead, an awning starts to melt. The awning is printed with the name of a hair salon, and the letters peel back from the heat. More people gather as the car fire blocks their way through the lot. The flames reach up under the window of the hair salon. Someone throws a rock at the window, but it bounces off. More people throw rocks, and the window shatters. People start chanting, "Burn. Burn."

A girl shakes her head at me like I'm a very large idiot. She says, "My friend works there." A rock whistles through the broken window, and something inside the salon crashes.

"I'm not doing anything," I retort.

An older guy steps in front of the crowd. "Stop!" He walks in front of us, waving his arms. "Just go home!" he says. "Go home!"

Someone shouts, "Get out of our way, old man!" Rocks fly. One must hit the older guy, because he grabs his shoulder.

The girl cries out, "No!"

Another rock hits him in the side and spins him around. He almost falls. The girl runs over to him and puts her arms over his head to shield him. Another man grabs them and pulls them back into the crowd.

People try to edge past the burning Mini, but the passage is narrow and some are repelled by the heat. More people pour into the lot, maybe thinking they can get through. I hear sirens and a loudspeaker telling us to clear the area. At the far edge of the crowd, a few uniformed police have formed a line.

One cop fiddles with his radio. Another shifts from foot to foot. I have no idea who these guys are, and whether they might know me. I turn so they won't be able to see my face.

"Clear the area. Clear the area."

If we go the way they want us to, we'll have to walk right past them. People form a barrier around the car. A guy with his hood pulled up hurls a rock at the police line.

People swarm, some trying to break through toward the cops, some trying to get past the car. Two guys start fighting, and some of the crowd circles around them to watch.

"Clear the area."

Where the hell do they think we can go?

The guy with the hood picks up another rock. I put my hand on his arm, but he pulls it away. Other guys chant at the police.

The color has gone from Nick's face. I'm not sure if it's because he's drunk or scared. Then a cheer lifts from the crowd. The police are retreating.

In an instant, the mood shifts. It's like in school, when the teacher leaves the classroom—now everyone's a renegade. New fights break out. The guy with the hood saunters around like he single-handedly turned back the cops. More likely, they're going for riot gear, I think, although I don't know why they don't already have it on. Others in the crowd pick up rocks and throw them after the police. I feel for the cops, but mostly I'm just glad none of them recognized me so no one will tell my dad. I'm so relieved, I start to laugh. Nick looks at me, stunned.

"It's okay," I say. "Let's get out of here."

Chapter Four

We manage to get past the Mini and back out onto the street and head back the way we came. Smoke rolls along the pavement. Alarms clamor from every store. Store windows are smashed, and people run out with armfuls of stuff. A guy emerges from an electronics store and jams a laptop under his jersey.

A couple of kids come out, each carrying one end of a huge box.

Nick whistles. "Flat screen, fifty-four inches."

"That's actually ridiculous," I say. "What do they say when they get home? 'Yeah, Mom, Dad, we were down at the riot and they were handing out free TVs'?"

Nick adds, "And they'll say, 'Did ya get us a Blu-ray? Go back and get us a Blu-ray.'"

The kids lumber off with their load. At a department store, a young woman peels out with three handbags. She gives one to another girl, who squeals, "Omigawd, it's Coach!" They dance around, hugging their purses.

It all feels more than ridiculous.

At a convenience store, Nick grabs my arm. "Come on," he says. "I need something to eat."

I'm surprised they're open, but when we go in, I see why. There's no one in sight. The workers must have fled, and the store has been trashed. The floor is ankle-deep with stuff shoveled off the shelves. Nothing good is left. The candy and chips are gone. The coolers are empty. There's a box of corn flakes busted open on the floor. The Slushee machine is on its side. Slush oozes like a neon-blue gunshot wound. Nick picks up a package of squashed hot-dog buns. In the bright lights of the store, his eyes are red and bleary from the booze.

"Yum," I say.

Painstakingly, he counts out a handful of coins and leaves them on the counter, rocking on his heels. Outside, he rips open the bag and starts to eat.

"You probably could have just taken those." I point to a boot print on the outside of the package. "I don't think they could sell them."

He shrugs. "If you want to steal something, go get me a flat screen." He crams another hot-dog bun in his mouth.

The streets are still packed. People stand around, either trashing stuff or watching it happen. Someone lit a trash can on fire, and a pack of guys stands around it as if it's a bonfire. As we walk past, Nick throws his bag of hot-dog buns in the fire. The plastic bag shrivels, and the buns go up with a satisfying *whoosh.* Nick tosses a smashed plastic patio chair toward the fire. It's from a restaurant. The place looks like it closed in a hurry—there are still dishes on some of the patio tables. The plastic chair spews a flume of black smoke and then starts to liquefy. The crowd cheers. Someone hands Nick a bottle of vodka, and he takes a long drink. The smell of burning plastic makes my eyes water. More trash gets tossed on. A planter on the patio railing catches, and the yellow flowers burst into fireballs.

I say to him, "I didn't know you were such a pyro." I reach over the railing and grab a plate off one of the tables. I Frisbee it into the fire. It smashes on the pavement and sends sparks flying into the air.

Sirens get close, and a fire truck bullies its way into the street. A line of riot cops follows the fire truck. I grab Nick's sleeve. "Come on!"

The pack of guys takes off with us. I spot the pizza shop Nick and I were at earlier. If we can get in, we can use the back door into the alley and get away from the cops that way.

I hear Nick say something about food as I kick out the rest of the window glass and climb over the sill. My feet crunch on broken glass. I turn to help Nick get through the window, but he's already in, along with about ten other people.

I don't know what they're doing. I just want to cut through. Someone flips the lights on, and they start throwing tables around. A girl puts her boot through the glass cooler and reaches in for the beer. I duck as a coffee mug whizzes past my ear. I make my way down a narrow hallway toward the back, pulling Nick with me. In the small prep area, he yanks open stainless steel fridge doors. I say, "What are you doing? We've got to get out of here."

He's weaving, completely wasted. He paws through industrial-size containers of olives and peppers. "I just need something to eat." He pulls out an immense container of pizza sauce, but it slips and he drops it. It opens on the floor and spews chunky red globs. Others crowd in with him. Someone turns on the spray faucet and hoses people. I turn to the back door.

That's when I see her, the girl who works here. She's almost completely hidden, huddled behind a stack of cardboard boxes. She's still in her apron. Her eyes are wide, her face ashen, and blood streams from her forehead. When she sees me looking at her, she crumples and starts to cry.

Chapter Five

It's not so much the blood as the look of absolute terror on her face that gets to me. How can she be so afraid of me? I hunker down beside her.

"Are you hurt?"

She recoils, as if she thinks I intend to harm her.

I say, "It's okay." Beside me on the floor is a big box of paper napkins.

I rip out a few napkins and dab the blood on her forehead. "I just want to help you."

Her eyes are wary, but she seems to relax.

I say, "So from the apron, I guess you're Abbi."

She nods and wipes her nose on her shirt sleeve. "Are you with them?" She gestures to Nick and the others trashing the kitchen.

I glance over at Nick. He's found a jar of peppers and a big spoon. He seems unaware that I'm no longer beside him. "No. We're, uh, I'm just trying to get away from the riot."

She nods. "They must have unlocked the door after they broke in."

I concentrate on her injured forehead. It won't do any good to tell her it was me who broke through the window. It won't make any difference if I tell her I didn't mean for all these morons to be in her shop. She'll just think I'm one of them.

She says, "I stayed to do dishes. My grandfather left. He didn't know it was going to get so bad."

"The guy with the tiger tattoo?"

She looks at me. "You've been here before?"

Before? Like when I would have been happy to tell her my name and not afraid she'd turn me in? I shake my head. "I guess, maybe. Not tonight though. Another time."

"They threw rocks and broke the windows."

As gently as I can, I wipe the blood away.

She gasps and pulls back.

I say, "There might be some glass in the cut." It's pretty deep. "You probably need stitches."

She looks like she might start to cry again. I say, "There are lots of ambulances." I glance again at Nick. He can't see me here under the counter. "You should get it checked."

She hugs her knees to her chest, and I see her hands are shaking. "I was scared to leave."

It hits me then—the mayhem out on the street, all the stuff people are doing—how scary it must be. All the stuff I did. "I know. It's crazy out there."

A huge plastic can hits the floor in front of us, and cooking oil erupts. It spatters the cupboard beside us and runs down it. People laugh. Another jar crashes on the floor, this one olives. Liquid geysers from the jar. Olives scatter and roll. People's feet smash the olives into ugly black smears. Then there's a huge crash, the sound of an entire tray of mugs breaking into bits.

Abbi's voice is small. "I just washed those."

There are more people crammed in behind the counter. I can't see Nick anymore, but he must be there. He wouldn't leave without me. I search for his feet among the others.

A woman's voice cries out, "Ew! He's going pee!"

Guys laugh. At the fridge door, I see a guy's jeans fall around his ankles and piss streams yellow from the bottom of the fridge.

Abbi's mouth tightens.

"Easy," I say.

"It's not right."

"I know. When you get to the ambulance, they'll tell the cops."

She raises one eyebrow. "You don't think I called the cops?" She pulls a phone from her pocket. "They said they're responding in priority order, so I know what that means."

She's probably right. Every store on the street is sounding alarms. The cops could be all night getting here. I say, "Right now you have to think about yourself. The rest of it is just stuff."

"Stuff?" Both eyebrows lift. "This is my grandfather's business. It's how we live."

"Yeah, but he must have insurance. He'd just want you to be safe."

The spray hose from the sink runs onto the floor and makes a greasy river of oil, smashed dishes, olives, and I don't want to know what else. I back away from the flow. Something digs into my back, a fire extinguisher bracketed under the counter. I shift away from it.

We both duck as a sauce container hits the floor.

She holds her phone out, and I hear it click.

She's taken a photo. The image is blurred. All it shows is the back of someone's legs and some indistinguishable figures in the background. She says, "They shouldn't get away with this."

In the photo, Nick is a big red blur.

She sneaks her phone out from the counter like she's going to take another picture.

I jump up. I'm not sure what to do, but I can't let her get a photo of Nick. I grab her by the wrists and pull her to her feet. "Come on," I say. "The back door. I'll go with you."

I have to push against all the people. It's like a nasty mosh pit—sweaty, hot and mean. I can't see Nick, only the wall of total strangers united in some weird angry ritual.

Abbi cries out, but I don't stop. I grip her hands as she holds on to my waist, and then bulldoze through the crowd.

"Hey!" People swear at me, push me. Someone side-arms me, but it bounces off my cheek. I don't care. I just want to get through. Abbi slips—I feel her collapse—but I hang on and drag her the rest of the way to the door. The door is barred from the inside, and I let go of her to lift the heavy steel bar out of the way. I throw myself against the push bar, and night air rushes in.

"We're out, Abbi." I turn to her.

She stands with her phone, focusing on the crowd.

I reach for the phone, but she pulls her arm free, raises it above her head and takes another picture. I grab her by a belt loop and haul her, stumbling, out of the shop. The door closes behind us with a *whump*.

Outside, the alley is black. The sudden stillness makes me blink. I can't see Abbi's face. I say, "I'm sorry." So sorry. "I just had to get you out of there."

She says, "It's okay."

The screen on her phone lights up to show the picture she just snapped.

"Ah," she says, pleased. "I got them." She holds the phone so I can see.

The image shows the walls of the shop strewn with every color of condiment, broken glass and dishes, the fridge door hanging off its hinges, water from a faucet spraying a random pattern against the ceiling. People's faces crowd the photo, jeering, laughing. One guy stares at the camera as he points his middle fingers. A girl ducks as something flies by her head. Some people have their heads turned. Some must have been moving when Abbi took the shot, because their faces are blurred. Clear and still, though, his head above the others, his red shirt like a beacon, one hand holding a jar of peppers up high almost like he's going to throw it, a spoon in the other, his face worried, like he's looking for someone, the image of Nick blares out of the photo.

Chapter Six

I don't know if stealing pickles can get someone arrested. Or dropping a jar of sauce. It only appears that Nick is with the rioters. But we *were* with them. I think about the overturned Mini, how the smoke burned my lungs. Right now it's like my lungs are on fire, because I can't breathe and I can't think. I broke into the shop, but it's Nick in the photo.

Will anyone believe that he's just in the wrong place at the wrong time? We threw some stuff. We set stuff on fire. Technically, maybe, Nick stole the stupid hot-dog buns. But he's not trashing the shop. He's not rioting. Would Abbi believe me, or would she think I'm covering for him? Would she think I'm covering my own ass?

"What's wrong?" Abbi asks.

The screen on her phone fades and I scroll my thumb to light it again. Nick's face shines out at me. If I delete the photo, then Nick isn't there. I could just make him disappear. I scan the screen. But I don't have this kind of phone, so I don't know where the icons are. My hand trembles.

Abbi takes the phone from me. She says, "Are you okay?"

How did it get this bad? Nick isn't crazy. I'm not. What is happening with everybody?

"I..." Words stick in my throat. If I tell her about Nick, that we've been friends for a really long time and that he's a really great guy and we didn't mean for this to happen, will she believe me? Because why didn't I just tell her the truth from the beginning?

No. Nick is screwed, but I am too. Now it's about damage control. From the light of the phone, I see that the cut on Abbi's forehead is bleeding again. With the tip of my finger I catch the rivulet before it runs into her eyes. "We need to get you to an ambulance."

She takes my arm, and together we pick our way down the dark alley. At the street, packs of people run past. A burned-out car smolders, its hulk like a blackened skeleton, the pavement around it charred and hot. Window glass pebbles the sidewalks. Cars are abandoned in the middle of the street, windshields smashed, doors kicked in.

A crowd rings around a couple of guys throwing punches. One of the guys is shirtless, his jersey stuffed into the waistband of his jeans. The other guy is smaller but landing the most punches. The shirtless guy swings, misses, catches one on the jaw. His head jerks back. The smaller guy nails him in the nose, and blood squirts out. A girl starts to wail. Another tries to get between the guys. Someone yanks her back.

"Crazy," I say, and steer Abbi around the throng.

"They're all idiots," she says. "They came down here looking for a fight."

"Jeez, Abbi."

She looks at me. "No, I don't mean you. You're a nice guy."

"Nice guys can't be idiots?"

"Those guys at the shop, they're not nice. There was nothing in there for them. We'd sold out of everything even before the end of the game."

I know, but I don't say it.

She continues, "Maybe they think it's fun, just harmless. But we can't open tomorrow. Maybe we can't open for a week. I don't know if my grandfather's insurance covers that. And who's going to clean it up?"

Guys run toward us. "Knife fight!"

Others have joined the fight. It looks like three guys have ganged up on the smaller guy. The shirtless fighter struts around like he's won. Yeah, except both his eyes are black, and he's got snot running down his chin. I don't see any knives, but it wouldn't surprise me. The fight draws people like a magnet. The crowd spans the street. Girls are up on guys' shoulders for a better view. People chant, "Fight! Fight!"

Abbi cries, "Oh!" Someone has elbowed past her, pushing her so she almost spins around.

In the few minutes we've been walking, the street has jammed with people. It's a different crowd now—edgy, wild. I hear sirens approaching.

I have to get Nick and get out of here.

Abbi's eyes are huge. People move in around us. It's like the crowd wants to consume us.

I say, "I'm right behind you. Keep walking. Don't stand still. Put your fists in front of your face and push."

She balls her hands into small fists. I stay at her back, but it's almost impossible. The crowd keeps pulling us apart.

I think about the kid with his mom I saw earlier, waiting for the washroom. I sure hope they got out while they could.

People, so many people, throw themselves against the crowd, and now I see why. A line of riot police advances from the end of the street toward us. Their shields and face masks reflect red and blue from the emergency vehicles alongside. The line acts like a giant squeegee, forcing people toward us. But the fight crowd blocks their way.

"They've got tear gas!"

People scream and climb over one another.

I pull Abbi close. "Turn around. Keep moving!"

But it's useless. Abbi stumbles, and I feel a police shield against my back. I bend to help Abbi up, and the cop pushes, hard. Now I'm on the pavement too, and an army of cops tromp past, their boots so close to our heads that I can see the treads. I put my arms over Abbi. The line passes and empties the street.

I touch Abbi's face. "Okay?" Her elbows are scraped and bleeding. Mine too, and my jeans are torn at both knees. Fresh blood runs down her face.

She nods, and her eyes fill with tears.

A paramedic runs over and kneels down beside Abbi. He starts working on her forehead, and she cries out.

"Glass?" he says.

She nods.

The paramedic talks into his handset, and an ambulance rolls into the street.

Abbi clutches my hand.

I say, "You're going to be okay."

It's like she's been holding it together, but now she crumbles. Her chest heaves as she sobs. The ambulance crew wants to strap her on a board, but she waves it away. She struggles to her feet. Two paramedics take her arms.

She looks at me and says, "I owe you."

I so wish this were some other time and place, when I could ask for her number, call her, take her somewhere normal, like to the beach or a movie. None of this tonight is normal. Nothing. And I don't know how I can make it up to her. I say, "No, you don't."

The paramedics lead Abbi to the back of the ambulance. Inside, people huddle on the benches. One guy has a bandage covering half his face. Abbi takes a spot by a guy wearing a tuxedo jacket over his jersey. “Thank you,” she mouths. And the doors close.

Chapter Seven

The street is strangely quiet. One or two blocks over, sirens volley off buildings and I hear the crowds, but where I am, right now, is like a concrete pod of aloneness. I'm suddenly aware of how tired I am. My jeans stick on my scraped knees. I pick a bit of gravel from the heel of my hand. For a small second, I think about going home, pouring a huge glass of water, taking it with me and collapsing in bed. I think about sleeping in tomorrow, all day, maybe. I'll call my boss and tell him I'm sick. I'll tell Dad I've got the flu. Maybe he'll bring me 7-Up. I don't love 7-Up, but he fills a glass with ice when he brings it to me, and it's good that way. I am so thirsty.

But first, I've got to go get Nick.

The pavement is covered with spilled trash, newspapers and plastic bags. An empty garbage bin rocks on its side. I don't know which direction the police line went.

At the street to Abbi's shop, groups of people knot around damaged cars. More guys fight. A girl dances with a store mannequin wearing tuxedo pants. The mannequin is missing its arms—and its jacket. People pour out of smashed storefronts. I don't know what's left to steal. In one store smoke detectors scream, and smoke snakes from the tops of the empty windows. Someone has set up chairs and a table from a restaurant in the middle of the street, complete with a bouquet of flowers in a vase.

As I walk toward the pizza shop, I see it is still crawling with people. Someone stands on the counter and yanks the TV from the wall mount. They can't be stealing it—they must just want to wreck it. In front, I push my way through a crowd watching two guys in muscle shirts fighting. Sitting on the curb, his elbows on his knees and chin in his hand, I find Nick.

I sit down beside him. "You okay?"

His eyes have that sunken look he gets when the booze wears off. "Where did you go?"

Nick's shirt is smeared with tomato sauce. The side of his face is swollen, like he ran into something or took a punch. But the way he asks it, there's no anger in it, just curiosity.

I think of the picture of Nick on Abbi's phone. I don't want to tell him about it. It's just a picture. What can the cops do with just a picture? I say, "There was a girl. I had to help her."

He gives me a long look and then says, "It doesn't matter."

I get up and reach out my hand. He takes it, and I haul him to his feet. He says, "Mia has been texting like a crazy woman. She's worn out the all-caps key on her phone."

"Did you tell her we got separated?"

"I told her we were waiting to get on the train platform."

I nod, relieved. "If we walk uptown, we might have a better chance of catching a bus."

A guy rushes past, pushing Nick so he almost falls into me. Then another. People spill out of the shop.

"What...?"

A smoke detector goes off. From the back of the pizza shop, smoke billows. People start cheering.

My stomach drops. "Oh no."

A guy vaults over the window ledge and into the street, wild-eyed and laughing. Another strolls through the front of the shop, dumping a can of cooking oil over the counter and floor.

I step toward the store. "They're torching it."

Nick grabs my sleeve. "What are you doing?"

"They can't do that."

"Don't be an idiot, Dan. Let's go."

I pull my arm free. "No." I push a guy out of my way. "Not this place." I throw myself over the window ledge. Inside, smoke makes me cough. The guy with the cooking oil shakes it onto the walls. My feet slither in the grease. I grab for the can and knock the guy to the floor.

I toss it out the window, and a stream of oil hits a couple. The girl screams and the guy swears. The guy on the floor scrambles to his feet and lunges for me. I sidestep him, and he crashes against the counter.

In the kitchen area, flames creep up the walls, throwing heat so that I have to hold my arm in front of my face. I pull the fire extinguisher from under the counter and fumble with the lever. Foam spurts from the nozzle, and I spray the flames, back and forth, knocking them down. Then someone has his hands on me. The back of my head hits the floor. Another guy jumps on my chest and starts punching me in the face. Someone's boot thuds into my ribs, and again. My breath catches. I swing blindly, hoping it connects. Pain rockets through my jaw, and I taste blood. My arms feel like lead, and I'm not sure if someone is holding me down or if I've just lost all my strength. Someone pulls me by the hair and slams my head into the floor. Around me, faces start to blur, laughing faces, jeering.

"Hit him!"

Another boot to the ribs, and this time I hear something crack.

I want to puke, but I don't because I'm afraid I'll choke. I try to breathe, but the pain in my chest is white-hot. I take tiny breaths, panting, drowning for air.

"Get off of him!"

I'm vaguely aware of a large red shape. The guy on my chest goes flying. Sirens now. The sound of boots. People running away. I spit a mouthful of blood. One eye doesn't want to open. For a second, everything looks red. I roll over onto my hands and knees. My ribs feel like knives. I get up on one foot, then the other.

Nick must have his mouth right up against my ear, because his voice ricochets in my head. "Hang on." He takes my arm over his shoulder. Pain blazes, but I can't cry out because that hurts too. Then cops, lots of cops, and I don't know what happens to Nick. Flashing red and white lights hurt my eyes, and then I'm in the back of an ambulance.

A shirtless guy on the street pounds on the door of the ambulance, hollering for a paramedic. His eyes are running, and he's coughing. Tear gas, maybe. A firefighter steps in front of him and the guy goes nuts. He gets in the firefighter's face and calls him a freaking queer. Beside me, a guy holds an ice pack against the side of his face. I wonder if he was one of the guys on top of me. Blood trickles from his nose. I doubt I did that to him. Maybe Nick did, or maybe he was in a different fight. How would anybody know?

Chapter Eight

I wake to the sound of *Jeopardy* at high volume. I'm at Nick's place. His grandmother is in her chair, eyes glued to the TV. Maybe she doesn't know I'm here on the couch, lying under a blanket. I'm using a toss cushion for a pillow and it smells suspiciously of Sebastian. On the coffee table is an empty glass—could be Sebastian's Pepsi glass from the game, or maybe someone brought me a drink of water. I could use another one. My throat is glued together. I get up on one elbow and immediately regret it. One side seizes with pain. I ease back down. I'm wearing just boxers, and the couch feels scratchy, but I don't have the energy to try getting up again.

Gram doesn't know about recording programs. She watches in real time. I enjoy the same mindless commercials over and over. Then Mia comes in, plunks her butt down on the coffee table and levels her stare at me.

I reach for my jeans on the floor by the couch to get my phone, but it hurts too much. I say, "What time is it?" My voice croaks.

"Ten thirty."

I groan. "I'm late for work."

"I phoned them for you." She is motionless. "Like you could go, in your condition. Nick went. I made him."

I don't know what time we got here. Nick was waiting for me when I came out of the emergency room at the hospital. Dad was too busy to leave work, not surprising, and the doctor said I had to go home with someone. So we called Mia, and she picked us up and brought us here.

Dad said he'd talk to me when he woke up. I don't know if he sounded more pissed or disappointed. I wish he was just pissed—it's easier to deal with.

My teeth feel furry. "Hey, Mia, could you maybe bring me a glass of water?"

She doesn't move.

"Please?"

Mia gets up, says something to Gram and returns with the remote. Standing beside me, she clicks through some channels. Riot police. A burning car. A guy carrying a computer box on his shoulder. At the news channel, she stops and sets down the remote.

The announcer's voice is irritatingly loud. Images from last night blast from the TV. They're showing video clips from people's cameras posted online. There's footage of the overturned Mini and the guy stuffing the rag into the gas tank.

I swallow. Mia stands watching me. I say, "Wild, huh?"

She crosses her arms.

Another shot captures two guys mugging for the camera in front of a shattered clothing store. In the background, people leave the store carrying armfuls of stuff. The news highlights the background figures to draw attention. Mia says, "What were you thinking, staying down there."

I'm not sure it's a question, but I give it a try. "Buses stopped running." This is true. Apparently, they couldn't get into the core, and even if they did, they couldn't get out. I say, "The lineup for the train took hours."

"You weren't in the lineup."

I need to text Nick. I don't know what he told his sister. I say, "We tried. We got caught in some stuff."

"You got caught," she says. I'm not sure she's repeating it or saying it.

I say, "In some stuff."

She points her finger at me. "Look at you, with your eye swollen shut and face one big bruise. Cracked ribs. You're lucky you didn't get knifed. People got knifed. It was a stupid game, and people lost their minds."

I know. I was in the emergency room with about fifty of them.

She continues, "You're really lucky nothing happened to Nick."

I guess I'm not getting a drink of water. I say, "Look, Mia, your brother is a big boy. We were having some fun.

He could have gone home. It's not like I forced him to stay down there."

She cocks her head. "Fun?" She points to the TV blaring images of the riot. "You call that fun? That was insanity."

"It was a few people doing insane stuff. Mostly it was just a lot of normal people."

"Normal people don't loot stores and trash cars."

"Actually, they do."

She looks at me hard. "A whole lot of normal people are getting arrested then. They're getting ID'd from their profile pictures."

I really could use some water. "Oh."

"Yes, oh. People are sending in clips and photos to the police."

"Did they just stand around taking pictures?"

"It worked out really well for you, stepping in." She rolls her eyes. "I can't imagine why more people didn't toss themselves in front of the rock throwers and pyromaniacs."

I think about Abbi, how afraid she looked when she thought I was going to hurt her. "You weren't there, Mia. You don't really know."

"I'm glad I wasn't there. I shouldn't have let Nick go, or you either."

"We're a bit too old for you to be babysitting us."

"We're family. Family cares about one another."

I feel my face redden. "But I'm not family. I should be at home."

"Okay, but you're like family. Sebastian pretty much thinks you're his brother." Mia's voice softens. "I do too."

On cue, the front door slams and Sebastian charges in. He's been at swimming lessons, judging by his dripping wet hair and the sodden towel he slings onto the end of the couch. Before I can tell him to stop, he launches himself at my chest. His knee finds the exact crack in my rib cage. I can't even cry out. My breath goes in and stops, and my eyes fill with tears. Mia plucks him off me and gingerly sets him on the couch by my feet. He settles back and watches TV.

She says to me, "I don't want to be your babysitter. I've got enough to worry about."

"You worry too much," I grunt.

"Maybe I'll stop worrying when people start being responsible for themselves." She looks pointedly at my bruises. "I'll bring you some water."

The front door opens and closes again, and I hear Mia say, "What are you doing home?"

Nick comes in. He's wearing his work shirt—he must have swabbed off the worst of the mess, but I can see where the tomato sauce splattered it. He looks like hell. Mia follows him.

"Nick, what happened?" she asks.

He glances at me. "I got fired."

Mia blinks. "Fired?"

Nick looks over at Sebastian. "Go play, okay, dude?"

Sebastian is glued to the TV.

Nick reaches over and jabs Sebastian's foot. "Sebastian, listen to me."

Sebastian pulls his foot away.

Mia puts her hands on her hips. She says to Nick, "Why? What did you do?"

Sebastian points to the TV and squeals, "Shoe Barn!"

Nick's head drops to his chest.

The clip is grainy, like it's been shot with a cell phone. The picture moves across the crowd to an overturned car. It's the Mini. In the background, Nick's red T-shirt stands out from the crowd of jerseys. He's posing for a picture, the one I have on my phone. His face is turned away, but his shirt is almost square to the camera, and yes, the name of the shoe store on his shirt is blindingly clear.

Mia's mouth hangs open. She says, "Is that you?"

Sebastian pushes himself off the couch. Without looking at anyone, he walks out of the room. I hear a bedroom door click closed.

Nick looks at his sister. "You can't wear your Shoe Barn shirt to a riot. Who knew? They want it back. I'll wash it. You can take it on your next shift."

She nods, stunned.

He turns to me. "You okay?"

"Nick."

He waves his hand. "No, I mean it. You need some breakfast or something? I'll make you some eggs."

"Jeez, Nick."

"How about French toast. I'll make us all French toast."

Nick's grandmother fumbles with the remote, and the TV goes quiet.

She struggles to her feet and crosses her cardigan across her chest. She looks at her grandson, her eyebrows furrowed, as if she's not sure who he is.

I reach out my hand to Nick. "You didn't do anything. You just posed for a picture. Did you tell them that?"

"They said they didn't need to discuss what I was doing. They said it was contentious or some such shit. They just asked if I wore my shirt outside of work. So I said yes. And yes, I knew it was against the rules. That was enough. They let me go." He peels out of his shirt. Without it, he looks soft, vulnerable. He says, "Okay, French toast it is. I hope we have canned peaches, because I love canned peaches on French toast."

I watch as he heads toward the kitchen. Mia looks at me. She raises her arms and lets them drop. She follows her brother out.

Chapter Nine

I haven't been off their couch all day. I've been glued to the news, dreading any more pictures. When Dad comes over, I drag myself into the kitchen. He's brought a pasta salad for supper. He's dressed for work. Sebastian crawls all over him until Nick hauls him to the table and dishes up the food. I pull my chair over to their computer.

My side hurts, but if I hunch and don't breathe, it's not too bad. Dad leans against the counter. As he looks at me, a muscle in his jaw clenches and unclenches. From the table, Nick looks back and forth from me to Dad.

I say, "I guess you've seen the clip."

He nods.

I say, "I guess we screwed up."

"Yup." He glances at Nick. "You want to go in with me?"

Nick's eyes get huge.

I start to jump to my feet, but pain shoots through my side and I sit back down. "Wait a minute. He didn't do anything."

Dad rubs his eyes. "If you were down there and didn't leave, then you were part of the problem. Both of you."

"You're going to charge thousands of people just for being there? We tried to help. They were going to torch the pizza place."

Dad gives me a hard look. "Something tells me that's not the whole story."

"Okay, maybe we got a little caught up. But Nick didn't do anything. He really didn't."

"And you? What about you?"

I swallow. "No. Nothing."

He sighs. "It was such a freaking gong show." He looks over at Sebastian. The boy is busy stabbing pieces of pasta onto his fork. Dad says, "I have to go to work. I'll come by and pick you up on my break."

Nick makes a choking noise.

Dad says to him, "I mean that I'll be by to take Daniel home." He looks at us both. "But you'd better hope there is nothing more incriminating out there."

I cover my face in my hands so he can't see how red it is.

Dad is gone for about one minute before Nick gets up. He doesn't say a word, just goes to his room.

Sebastian climbs down from his spot at the kitchen table. "You're a hero, right?" He wanders over to where I'm sitting. He carries his plate with one hand, careening with it half-tipped so that the pasta slithers to the very edge. I grab it from him and set it by the computer. Sebastian stands beside me, cramming his mouth full of pasta salad while he stares at the monitor.

"A hero? No one is a hero, Sebastian. Heroes don't exist in real life."

He has so much in his mouth that his nostrils flare as he gulps down the food. He says, "Mia said you might be on the news."

At the hospital last night, a camera crew wanted to interview me but I refused. They got a shot of my messed-up face before I slammed the car door on them.

My own plate is untouched. I click on a video site showing a news interview with Abbi. I saw it on TV earlier. Abbi's forehead is bandaged, and she has dark circles under her eyes. They're standing in front of the boarded-up pizza shop. Nearby, people sweep a mess of tipped garbage, newspapers, bottles and cans. The interviewer asks Abbi, "When will you be back open for business?"

Abbi shakes her head. "We have to get the repairs done first. It's pretty tough finding a crew right now. Contractors aren't even returning our calls."

"Not to mention the expense."

Abbi looks like she's struggling to compose herself. "The owner, my grandfather, he's not sure he wants to reopen." She touches her forehead. "He feels like it's his fault that it happened, that he wasn't here to protect his property."

The interviewer says, "Or you."

Abbi looks away.

“It must have been terrifying,” the interviewer clucks, and then the shot moves to another interview.

No photo. Maybe the police have it and are hanging on to it. My stomach tightens. I leave the clip and go back to the riot images people sent in. Arson. Unlawful assembly. Mischief. Participating in a riot. I watch news footage of people coming out of the police station. Some look dazed. Some laugh.

Sebastian picks out a miniscule piece of green pepper from the salad and flicks it onto the edge of his plate. He says, “You are too a hero, because you beat up the bad guys.”

I rub my sore side. “That’s kind of subjective.”

He looks at me.

I say, “Like, whether a guy is bad or good. It depends on how you see it.”

Sebastian thumps his foot against the leg of the chair. *Thud. Thud. Thud.*

Arson. Unlawful assembly. If Abbi sends in the picture she took of the people trashing her shop, Nick is screwed. It's so unfair. Nick didn't do anything. He threw a bottle and set some garbage on fire. Big deal. Other people were doing so much more.

Mischief. Participating in a riot. Nick and his giant-sized red shirt will stand out in any photo or video clip. I click through more images. People who want to nail someone have an easy target with Nick.

No images of me, so far. I'd lose my job too. And then there's my dad's reputation.

Thud. Thud.

I put my hand on Sebastian's shoulder. "Stop kicking my chair, okay?"

"I don't like the salad."

"Really?" I glance at his plate. "You sure ate enough of it."

"It has green peppers."

Dad puts green peppers in everything. Onions and green peppers. "So?"

"Maybe Mia will make me something when she comes home."

Thud. Thud. The sound makes my head ache.

"Or maybe you'll eat your pasta and leave everyone alone."

He looks at me and blinks. "Your dad is mad at you."

"He'll get over it."

"Mia is too."

"It that right?"

Thud. Thud. "Mia says you aren't a hero." *Thud.* "She says just because you didn't show up in the photos doesn't mean you weren't doing stuff."

My eyes burn from looking at so many images. I say, "Mia says that, does she?"

Thud. "She says you don't want to go on the news because then people will recognize you."

I give him a shove. "Your sister should be an effing rocket scientist, she knows so much."

His lower lip quivers.

I push myself to my feet, ignoring the pain that clamps my torso. I grab his plate and dump the food into the garbage. "Too bad you don't like green peppers."

Tears slide down his cheeks, and the anger ebbs out of me.

"Jeez, Sebastian, I'm sorry, okay?"

He doesn't want me to know he's crying. His face is all screwed up with trying to hold it in.

I am such a dick. I say, "You want a sandwich? How about a bologna sandwich?"

His chest shudders as he gathers himself. "I don't like bologna."

"How can you not like bologna?"

"It's sticky."

I say, "You've never had the kind I make."

I reach into the fridge for the mayo but can't lift my arm to bring it out. "Uh, dude, you're going to have to help."

He wipes his nose on his shirt sleeve and clambers up for the jar. I flip bread out onto the counter. I trowel mustard and mayo onto the sandwiches.

He says, "Mia makes them like that, and they stick."

"Have a little faith." I assemble the sandwiches and push one toward him. As usual, he turns it upside down. Gently, I turn it in his hand. "Mustard has to be on top."

He takes a tiny bite and chews. Then he takes a bigger bite.

"See?"

He takes a huge bite and nods.

I say, "My mom taught me that."

He reaches for another sandwich and carefully positions the mustard on top. After a while he says, "Is Nick going to jail?"

My own sandwich forms a gluey glob partway down my throat. I avoid Sebastian's gaze. "He won't go to prison," I say. I hope he doesn't hear the quake in my voice. "You think we should make a sandwich for Gram?"

"She likes cornflakes."

"For supper?"

He shrugs. "Mia says Gram is doing her best and to cut her some slack."

"Your sister knows. Go get the cornflakes."

Chapter Ten

My phone wakes me. I peel one eye open to see that my room is still dark. I fumble with the phone to see who is calling.

"It's three AM, Nick."

There's nothing from his end, and for a second I think it's a pocket dial. But then he speaks. His voice is cracked and shaky. "I'm going in."

I force my eyes to unstick. "What happened?" My stomach rolls. "Is there something else up? Did somebody post another picture?"

"No."

I let out a relieved sigh. "So that's good. You don't have to do anything."

"Yeah, I do. People at work know."

I yawn. "They can't prove it's you."

He's quiet too long.

"You didn't admit anything, did you?"

Another silence. "People at work are pumping Mia about why I got fired. They knew I was going down to watch the game. They know some idiot wore his Shoe Barn shirt. They're treating Mia like crap. How is she responsible?"

"Maybe she should just quit."

He snorts. "Like it is so easy to get another job."

"No one knows anything, Nick."

"They know it's me, Daniel. They've already posted online."

"They only know you posed for a photo, that's all. Just let this blow over."

"I can't. I'm going in."

I rub my eyes and try to regain some sense of alertness. "We should talk in the morning. These things always look rough in the middle of the night."

"It's plenty rough, Daniel." Another pause. "People are saying stuff online."

I roll out of bed and start heading toward the computer. Dad's bedroom door is open. He's still at work. "You took down your account, didn't you?"

"It's on Mia's."

Shit, shit, shit. I log in.

Nick says, "Even Sebastian's getting flak. One of his buddies called him a loser for being my brother."

I go to Mia's Facebook page. There must be fifty posts.

I feel bad for you. You shouldn't have to deal with this.

Your parents didn't know where he was going? I never would have let him go down there.

Hopefully the kiddy gets arrested and does real time.

He deserves everything he gets.

Your brother is a @# thug.*

I want to come to your house and rip the shit out of it.

Your brother is gay.

You should move.

You losers.

Idiot.

Moron.

Douchtard.

Nice. I say, "Who are these people anyway?"

"Used to be friends, I guess."

"Has Mia seen this?"

"Oh yeah." He's gets quiet.

Shit.

I can barely hear him. He says, "People she's known all through school are cutting her loose. Her best friend isn't returning her calls."

"Why? This has nothing to do with her."

Nick says, "And Sebastian told my parents."

My stomach does a one-eighty. "Oh."

Total silence.

"Nick?"

He sounds like he's crying. "I don't want them with me when I go in. I don't want their faces plastered all over the news like they're criminals."

"You're not a criminal." I struggle for a clear thought. "You should talk to my dad. He knows you. He knows you didn't..."

"Daniel, listen to me. I'm going in."

A new kind of pain wrings my chest. If he admits to taking part in the riot, he may as well turn me in too.

Nick says, "And my parents know me. Or they thought they did."

"I didn't mean they didn't."

"People are right about me. I'm a loser."

"Why are you talking like this? You didn't do anything."

"I did though." I hear him suck in a breath. "All those people at the pizza place, they were going to run past. I called them. I said there was food."

"Ah. That's why you're guilt-tripping."

"Don't pass this off, Daniel. I waved them in."

"But you didn't do..."

"Stop saying that. They wouldn't have been in there except for me."

"Well, or except for me. I was the one who broke out the window."

"Well, there are no pictures of you. It's like you weren't even there."

I'm ashamed to ask it, but I have to. "So your parents don't know about me?"

"No. They were a bit more focused on their screwup anarchist son."

"Nick, do they know you were in the pizza place?"

"They know everything, Daniel. I can't stand what this is doing to them. Mia is a total mess. Sebastian thinks I'm going to prison. Gram was crying. Everyone was crying. I am so done with this bullshit. I don't care what they charge me with, I just want to get people to lay off my family."

They know. Everyone knows.

I say, "So, where did you say I was?"

There's a long pause, and when he speaks, his voice is thick with resentment. "This really is all about you."

"Nick."

"No, it is. You don't want me going in because it will make you look bad. You're afraid people will see that the hero isn't so wonderful after all."

"I'm not parading around like a hero. People are making that up just like they're making you look bad."

"Mia hates your guts. I told them you ditched me for a girl."

I think about my promise to her. "But I had to."

"You had to? You had to just bugger off? You had to leave me and go with some girl—in the middle of a riot?"

"Yes." He may as well know. "She was taking pictures. I had to get her out of there."

"Pictures. Of us?"

I pause. "She didn't get one of me."

"No, of course she didn't."

"Nick, I didn't mean for any of this to happen."

His voice is like ice. "But she got a picture of me?"

I sigh. "Yes."

"There's a picture of me inside the pizza place?"

"Yes."

"With all the rioters?"

"Nick, I don't know."

"Just tell me!"

"Okay, yes! But she hasn't posted it—"

He interrupts, "There's a picture of me rioting inside the pizza place. You let me go all day yesterday knowing it's out there? It's what your dad would call incriminating, wouldn't you say? When the hell were you going to tell me?"

I try to think of something to say, but it all sounds so lame.

He says, "You weren't going to tell me."

"She hasn't posted it. Maybe she lost her phone. Maybe it got deleted by accident."

"Maybe you just didn't want me turning myself in."

"I don't know what you want me to say."

"Yeah. Right. Don't worry about it."

"Nick, I'm sorry."

"I'll say you ditched me because I was being a moron. Nothing will stick to you."

I try to apologize again, but he's already disconnected.

Chapter Eleven

My alarm clock won't stop beeping. I hammer it with my fist, but the damn thing keeps going off. Then I realize the sound is coming from outside—a truck is backing down the street. Nine AM. I crack open the blinds and look down.

It's a network television truck, and now it's stopped out front. A couple of people in suits stand on the sidewalk. I recognize one, the same woman who interviewed Abbi.

What did Nick tell them? I pull on my clothes. In the bathroom, I yank my fingers through my hair and flatten the worst knots. Dad's door is closed, thank goodness. I don't want these bozos waking him up. I take the stairs down two at a time. When I open the front door, every head turns.

A guy points a video camera at me and calls, "Daniel Brysan?"

I put my hand in front of the camera, and the guy lowers it. I say, "It's pretty obvious you know who I am."

The woman runs up. She's almost breathless. She wrestles into a jacket as someone flicks a makeup brush over her face. She smiles at me, and her teeth are shiny white. "Hi, I'm Megan Liu. Gosh, you were not easy to find."

The guy with the camera shifts around, and now I'm looking into the sun. It makes my head hurt.

She says, "We'd like to get some footage, if that's okay. We'll run it tonight."

The makeup person comes toward me with a brush. I step back. "Uh, no, it's not okay."

Megan Liu is handed a microphone, and she does a quick sound check. "No makeup, I agree. People will want to see what they did to you." She makes a clucking sound.

That's not what I meant, of course. She nods at the camera guy and turns to face me. "That was incredibly brave, taking on the rioters. What made you step up when so many others just stood by?"

So this isn't about Nick. I stammer, "Uh, how did you find me?"

She lowers the mic. "Someone in the ER heard your name and gave it to us."

My eyebrows shoot up. "One of the nurses?"

"No, no. It was a person waiting to be admitted. He must have heard your name get called. I'm not really sure." She smiles. "Take your time. Relax." She puts her hand on mine. She has perfectly manicured nails. "Tell me what happened that night."

I say, "Some people, they got out of control. I just tried to stop them."

"And they turned on you?" She lifts the mic again.

"Yeah." I touch the side of my face. "There were too many of them. I couldn't really fight back."

She asks me about my injuries, so I tell her. She stays quiet and lets me talk. Someone hands her a tablet, and she glances at it.

She says, "You're friends with this young man?" She shows me the tablet. It's the video clip of the overturned Mini, the one with Nick posing. He's been highlighted.

So it is about Nick. I look at the camera, suddenly aware of the light on top of it. The camera guy has been recording all of this.

She says, "The young man in this clip turned himself in earlier today."

I swallow. "He didn't do anything."

"He apologized to his family and the city."

I stand without speaking.

She says, "So you and he were down at the game together?"

"Yes, but he didn't do anything." I want to punch the guy with the camera.

"Daniel, you're being heralded as a hero for preventing the arson of Nel's Pizza Shop. The owner's granddaughter, Abbi, says that earlier, you were in the shop and helped her escape from rioters who basically destroyed the place."

My breath catches, and my brain scrambles for a thought.

"In the shop? I don't think so. She must be mixing me up with someone else."

Megan Liu looks at her notes. "She recognized a photo of you we shot outside the hospital as you got out of the ambulance." She reads, "'I want to thank him for everything, for saving the shop, for helping me get away from the rioters.'"

I shake my head, fast. "No. That was someone else."

"She said she was trapped in the back of the shop and actually feared for her life." She refers to her notes again. "'He was kind and brave when everyone was so cruel.'"

"That's nice, but it wasn't me."

"So you were with your friend the whole time?"

Did he say we got separated? It's like a steel band tightens around my chest. "We…a big group of people, we were trying to get away from the riot." I force myself to make eye contact with her. "We got separated for a while."

"How did rioters get in to Abbi and her grandfather's shop?"

"I have no idea."

"How did you get in?"

"I think we went in the door. It might have been the window. I can't remember."

She says, "Do you still say that your friend was not involved in the riot?" She shoves the microphone closer toward me.

I take a deep breath. "He didn't do anything. There's no evidence. Nothing is going to stick."

She grabs back the microphone. "Your father is a police officer, isn't that right?"

I sigh. "Yes."

"Does your father say there will be no charges laid?"

"I'm not sure he knows."

"If your friend didn't do anything, and if there's no evidence, why do you think he turned himself in?"

I know the camera asshole is zooming in on my face right now. "People are pulling all this vigilante crap and saying stuff, and it's scary, you know? People are dumping on his family." I pause. "He posed for a freaking picture, so what does that make him, an arsonist? A vandal? How about a poser? Yeah, he's a poser, that's it. Maybe turning himself in makes him feel tough, like he has some control. Leave him alone and leave his family alone. He doesn't deserve any of this."

Chapter Twelve

I went over to give Sebastian my jersey. He accepted it but didn't put it on. Nick wasn't there. Sebastian said he was out dropping off resumes. Apparently Nick can't keep his phone on because he's getting hate texts. I'm still waiting for him to call me. Maybe he believes all the postings online. They play over and over again in my mind.

He called him a poser. Some friend.

I know these guys. Nick doesn't do anything unless DANIEL BRYSAN tells him to.

Obviously DANIEL BRYSAN is covering his ass.

Nice, really nice. Maybe DB needs to get shit-kicked again.

He should do the time, not Nick.

DB = Douche Bag.

And then there's this post. I recognize the user name. It's from Mia: *He is trying to help his friend. You guys sound like the idiots.*

Ever since the news interview, I've been waiting for a photo to show up. Maybe I should be glad that nothing does. But I don't feel glad. I feel done.

And now Dad's awake. His coffee is cold on the table in front of him. He rubs the stubble on his chin and turns off the news. When I can't stand the silence anymore, I say, "I'm sorry, Dad."

"Anyone with half a brain knows you're lying."

He's looking at me the same way he looks at my mother. It empties me.

"That's not who I am, Dad."

"You can't just say stuff and hope it becomes real."

"I know that now." I gather a breath and say, "We were in the shop, both Nick and I. We were running away and cut through."

"Running from the police?"

"From the riot," I say. I look him in the eye. "And the police."

"The shop was closed?"

I nod.

"So you broke in?"

"Break and enter. Yes. I should have turned myself in when Nick did. We should have done it sooner. I cut him loose and nothing I say changes that."

Dad seems so much smaller all of a sudden. He slouches back in his chair.

"It was crazy, Daniel. People were throwing stuff at us—beer cans, bottles. Even the guys on horses got it. One thug threw a full beer bottle in front of a horse and then laughed when it shattered and cut the horse's legs." He gets up and starts pacing. "I wanted to pound the guy. I wanted to smash my fist in his face. But no, we can't do that because we're supposed to stay calm. So we warned people over and over again to get out. We gave them every chance to leave. Then when they didn't and when we used tear gas, they called us pigs."

I think about the guy at the ambulance going apeshit on the firefighter.

He continues, "They destroyed property. They terrified families with little kids. You did." He jabs his finger at me. "You. God help anyone with a real emergency that night, because we were all downtown getting spit at and kicked and generally shit on. And now you're sorry?" He throws his hands in the air. "If there weren't all these thousands of pictures, I wonder if anyone would be apologizing."

Chapter Thirteen

The windows of the pizza shop are boarded up so that even at noon, the interior is dark. Debris covers the floor. The beer cooler is gone. Maybe it got taken that night and is sitting on a street corner somewhere. On the spot where it used to be, the flooring looks like new. Everywhere else, greasy black soot coats the floor. The walls are full of holes, and the place stinks like damp wallboard.

"Abbi?"

My feet stick on the flooring as I make my way to the back of the shop. The alley door is propped open, and I find Abbi dragging out a box of water-soaked paper towels. Her face is streaked with dirt. On her forehead, there's a square bandage. She looks up and says, "The famous Daniel Brysan." She wipes her hands on her jeans. "This time I left the front door unlocked for you."

"I didn't expect you to be happy to see me."

She shrugs. "After that thing on the news? I didn't expect to see you at all."

I nod. "I guess not."

She scrapes a smashed olive from the bottom of her shoe.

I say, "You didn't post the picture."

She looks at me. "I knew I'd seen you before, but I couldn't remember from where. But when I looked at my picture, I remembered the big guy in the red shirt, that he'd been at the shop earlier, and that you were with him."

"Nick." I nod. "But there were other people in the shot though. You could have posted the photo so they'd be identified."

Again, she shrugs. "I knew he was your friend. I thought I'd help him out because you helped me."

"Thanks…"

She interrupts. "You were covering for yourself. But whatever, I owed you." She waves her hands as if to brush it off. "We're even."

"No, we're not. Not even close."

Her eyebrows furrow.

I say, "That night, I did some stuff I'm not proud of. Nick did too, but mostly it was me." My throat wants to clamp up. "I broke in here hoping to escape the riot, and all the rest of them followed. They thought I meant to trash the place. They probably wouldn't have been here except for me."

She crosses her arms. She looks like she wants to say a few things. I hold up my hand to stop her. "But I'm not saying sorry. My dad says actions speak louder than words." I reach into my pocket and hand her an envelope. "It's a bank draft. Everything I've got."

When I told him what I was doing, my dad said he'd find another buyer for his old truck.

She opens the envelope, and her eyes widen.

I say, "I got you a good deal with a construction company I work for. Or used to work for. I'm not sure if they'll keep me. Probably depends on what I'm charged with."

She finds her voice. "So you turned yourself in?"

"Just before I got here. You can see it on the news tonight. Megan Liu was at the station and filmed about a year of footage."

One of my boss's company trucks pulls into the alley. A guy gets out and starts directing a huge garbage bin into the space right behind the shop.

Abbi looks at me, questioning.

Another truck shows up, and a crew of guys gets out and starts unloading a stack of drywall from the back. Two of the guys shoulder a roll of industrial-weight vinyl flooring.

Abbi seems totally stunned. She blinks as one of the workers hefts the box of ruined paper towels into the dumpster.

I say, "Don't worry. We cleared all this with your grandfather."

We follow the crew into the shop. Workers pry off wrecked wallboard while others begin repairing the window.

Another gets a scraper and starts peeling away the old flooring.

I pick up a broom. I can't sweep—it hurts my ribs too much—but I can push the debris into a heap. Abbi gets a wheelbarrow and starts loading it.

I say, "I really am sorry, Abbi."

She says, "I don't think you are evil, or your friend either."

"He's not. Nick is the greatest guy."

She pauses. "You made a difference for us that night. It doesn't matter why you did it."

I stop her. "Don't thank me."

"I wasn't going to."

My face reddens.

She laughs. "Actions speak louder than words, right?" She goes to the counter and rummages through the mess to find a pencil and scrap of paper. "My number." She writes it and hands it to me. "If you're looking for a job, we might need someone to help in the shop.

My grandfather would feel better with a bit more manpower."

I look at the piece of paper. "I appreciate it, I do. But if it's all right with you, I'd like Nick to get the job."

Abbi says, "Does he know anything about food?"

"Nick?" I smile. "He can cook, I guess. He knows more about eating. But you probably won't have any more trouble, not while he's working."

She drops a shovelful into the wheelbarrow. She says, "He should call me."

"I'll give him your number."

She smiles a little. "You can keep it too."

I grin.

"Don't thank me," she says.

"I wasn't going to," I say. I reach over and wipe a smudge of dirt from her cheek.

Diane Tullson wrote *Riot Act* after the Stanley Cup riots in Vancouver. She has written a number of other Soundings titles, including *Lockdown*, *Sea Change* and *Riley Park*.